The Prison Diaries of

Gaspard Renouille

By

Michael Little

First published by Barny Books. All rights reserved

ISBN No: 978.1.906542.14.6

Publishers: Barny Books
Hough on the Hill,
Grantham,
Lincolnshire,
NG32 2BB

Tel: 01400 250246
Email: Barnybooks@hotmail.co.uk

For Aengus

THE PRISON DIARIES OF GASPARD RENOUILLE

L'Oubliette Prison

Lasciate ogni speranza, voi qu'intrate

Dante: Divina Commedia canto 1

719896
Renouille Gaspard
Daylight Robbery

Gaspard

Prison isn't all it's cracked up to be. A nice long rest, with nothing to do but eat three meals a day and doze on your bed? Forget it. After a day or two doing nothing you'd be desperate for some distraction and time would drag at your feet like wading through duckweed on stilts. You'd start thinking of all the nice things you could do if you had your freedom. Chasing butterflies and sitting in the sun with your mates at the village pond. Snacking on juicy bugs and bluebottles, playing leapfrog with the little ones or singing in the choir at night. No, it's best not to think of the past; far better to find something to occupy your mind because, that's where you will find freedom. Look for something interesting that can be done every day and never gets finished, so that tomorrow and the day after, you are still looking forward to the next day's work, with no prospect of ever finishing, but still enjoying doing it. Like cooking.

That's what I do, and I love my work.

My name is Gaspard Renouille. I was sent here for robbing a drunken newt. It wasn't my first crime; there were many robberies, and for a long time stealing was the only thing I knew.

It wasn't that I'd had a deprived childhood; I grew up in my parents' restaurant and had all the food I wanted, but I was lazy. I didn't go to school. I wrote rude words on the wall and hung around with a bad lot.

nobody could read them as my spelling was so bad

My mother, Madame Gigi used to say, "He just needs love and attention".

My father, chef Gaston said, "He needs a blooming good hiding".

The gendarmes all agreed, "He needs locking up".

In the hope that I might get a respectable job my Papa took me to the Institute of Accountants to sit the entrance exam.

Accountants are clever people who make a lot of money preventing silly people from wasting theirs'.

The entrance exam was very hard.

I had to add up an enormous sum (100 + 100). It was too much for me.

And so ended Papa's hopes of a decent future for his problem child.

After being rejected by the Foreign Legion for having flat feet, I took to a life of crime.

I joined a gang, and had a picture of my favourite meal tattooed on my chest. My new friends all admired me and gave me the honorary nickname 'Papillon Renouille'.

The gang admired their leader's tattoo

Our gang was notorious for jumping out of bushes and robbing people of their money. I quickly became their leader and masterminded a lot of successful robberies.

The gendarmes couldn't catch me because I was careful to go in disguise. They put up posters, and offered a reward for my capture.

It couldn't last, of course, and one day I was caught and, sent to jail.

A lady out for a walk with her children spotted me breaking into a house, and recognising my trademark chef's trousers, called the police on her cell phone.

There was no escape, and soon I found myself in court facing a stern magistrate intent on teaching me a lesson.

He sent me to a jail that was notorious for its hard discipline and bad food. Being lazy by nature, I thought I'd have an easy time in prison if I could work in the kitchens. After all, I'd grown up in a restaurant and knew a thing or two about food.

When I saw the state of the prison kitchen, I was horrified.

The cook was a dirty toad who never bothered to peel the potatoes or do the washing up, and the kitchen was a disgrace. Worst of all, the brute hated cooking, and complained all the time about his hard luck being condemned to work in the kitchen, when he could have been scratching himself in the dried mud puddle in the prison exercise yard.

I saw my chance, and volunteered to relieve him of his duties and take over the cooking myself.

That's when I found my true mission in life:

I would cook. I would be a great cook, a great and famous cook.

That was my dream, and I set about achieving it at once.

I cleaned the kitchen, ordered new ingredients for the sauces, and made my first spectacular banquet to which I invited the Governor and his Chief Accountant.

They couldn't believe the transformation I had made to the gloomy kitchen, and when they tasted my *Papillon en croûte* they knew that something marvellous had happened in their prison, and that I was responsible for it.

10

The Governor helped me transform the sloppy old eating hall into a smart restaurant where all the inmates could enjoy their food in comfort, and the Chief Accountant agreed to pay for the exotic ingredients I needed for my sauces. The restaurant was a great success, and even old Toady the ex-cook looked forward to dinnertime and made an effort to scrape himself down before joining the other prisoners at table. Each morning I awoke eager to get to my kitchen and start on preparations for breakfast, lunch and dinner, and my last thoughts at night were my plans for the next day's menus. And in this way time raced by.

The Governor

The Governor was a wise old frog, and very optimistic about his chances of reforming the ne'er-do-wells in his charge. He believed that all frogs, toads, newts and lizards in his prison could be made into responsible members of society if they could only be taught to look after one another, and give up their selfish ways. He called it 'Mutual Support', which was his way of saying 'Look after your mates, and they will look after you'. This was a novel idea to most of my fellow prisoners, whose only thought was to rob their mates, if they could.

Morning in the prison commenced with a Roll Call, to make sure that nobody had jumped over the wall and legged it. This was the job of the Chief Accountant, who made us all line up in the prison yard while he counted us. Then he turned to the Governor, saluted, and said, "All present and correct, sir." That was the Governor's cue to start his daily lecture on his favourite improving topic, 'The Crime of Selfishness.'

On this occasion he had thought of a novel way of demonstrating how we all suffered if we allowed one of our number to suffer.

He called it the Domino Effect, and this is what he did.

13

We were ordered to stand in line one behind the other until all the prisoners formed a great circle around the muddy pond in the middle of the yard. The Governor made us shuffle up close to one another until we were almost touching, and then without any warning, he pushed over the prisoner at the head of the line. The startled frog reeled backwards and knocked over the one behind, who also was propelled into the arms of the next one, and so on until the entire circle of frogs, toads, newts and lizards lay thrashing about in the dust. Fights broke out among those who blamed each other for their injuries, and it took some time for the Chief Accountant to restore order.

The Governor then delivered the Moral.

"If the second in line had kindly caught the prisoner in front of him and prevented him from falling, then all this would not have happened, and you wouldn't have suffered." We weren't too sure of the logic of this, and anyway, some of us enjoyed an excuse for a fight.

The Governor was not only a wise old frog, he was a patient one, and not easily put off by the apparent failure of his lesson in 'Mutual Support'.

The following day he repeated the scenario in the prison yard, and we found ourselves in the same position standing close together in a big circle, so that there was no beginning or end to the line. We were anticipating being floored in the same way as on the previous day, but the Governor had a surprise in store for us.

"Sit down!" he commanded, and we obeyed. Everyone sat in the lap of his neighbour to the rear, and for a few moments we were supported in comfort by each other, astonished at the effect of our co-operation.

It couldn't last, of course, because a slippery newt slid off his seat and the whole circle collapsed in a heap on the ground. We all laughed until we had tears in our eyes, and struggled to re-create the experience. The morning passed hilariously while we tried to perform tricks like 'the walking armchair', until the entire circle fell into the prison pond, where a spontaneous display of synchronised swimming was improvised to the delight of the Governor, who then felt no need to lecture us on the Moral, as we had obviously learned to enjoy the benefits of 'Mutual Support'.

Beauregard Buffo

I made many friends among my fellow prisoners, and got to know
their likes and dislikes, their dreams and ambitions, and the crimes
that had led them here.

Apart from mugging and swindling, there were other anti-social
offences, which could get you a spell in prison, such as 'Aggressive
Snoring', 'Being Blue', and 'Being Ugly'.

My unfortunate neighbour, Beau Buffo, in the cell next to mine had
committed the latter offence. The judge had sent him to prison
because he was so ugly it made peoples' eyes sore and watery just
looking at him. Beau and I became friends when I discovered his
unusual hobby.

Beau kept himself to himself, spending long hours in his cell and
refusing to join the others for daily exercise in the prison pond.

He had grown shy of company due to his sad experience of people wincing and making disgusted faces when they looked at him, and so he avoided his fellow prisoners, sitting alone at the dark end of the restaurant at meal times.

One day, a butterfly flew through the bars of his cell window, and finding a dark, dry corner, laid its eggs, and folding its wings together as if in prayer, it died. It was later discovered by Beauregard as he was counting the bricks in the wall to pass the time. Beau gently prised the butterfly's wings apart and marvelled at the vivid colours and patterns that shone back at him from this jewelled insect. The thought of adorning himself had never occurred to the homely toad, but seeing the beauty of the glowing wings, he licked the insect with his sticky tongue and glued it to his chest, where it remained for all to see.

17

I spotted it at once and complimented him on his choice of ornament, for I also had a butterfly, a tattoo on my chest that had given rise to my nickname 'Papillon Renouille'. We became friends, and although he was a toad, we had a lot in common. Our favourite food was grubs, and in particular, the caterpillars of butterflies.

As time passed, the eggs in Beauregard's cell developed into caterpillars, and finally into butterflies which went on to reproduce themselves, until Beau's cell was all a-flutter with thousands of beautiful butterflies, and nurseries squirming with caterpillars. Beau suddenly found himself in demand, and very popular with the other inmates. He started to smile, shyly at first, and then with growing confidence, until his smile lit up his ugly face and made everyone happy to look at him. The tender caterpillars and crunchy pupae, which he supplied to the kitchens, became the mainstay of my menus, and the butterfly wings were eagerly collected by his neighbour, the milliner and poisoner, Jorge Borge.

Jorge Borge

Jorge was an Amazonian blue poison-arrow frog who was sent to prison for being blue, and for poisoning his landlady by spitting in her drink. He claimed that he had only taken a surreptitious swig of her drink when she wasn't looking, and his naturally poisonous saliva had unfortunately done for her. Nobody believed him, however, when it was discovered that he owed her a year's rent, and she had threatened him with the police if he didn't pay.

Jorge missed his home in the Amazonian jungle and did his best to recreate a forest effect in his cell. He collected coloured moss and mud from the prison pond and draped it over the bare bricks. Twigs and feathers added to the effect, and soon he felt quite at home.

He was constantly on the lookout for ways of improving his surroundings. He spent many hours in the prison library poring over copies of the fashion magazine 'Nouvelle Vague', and was particularly impressed by the work of *Gino Renouille, the exciting young Parisian designer. 'If Gino can become famous for his dresses and shoes,' he thought, 'maybe I could become famous for designing hats'. Back in the jungle, all the members of his tribe had sported feathery headgear, so Jorge felt that he had a natural advantage in the millinery line of work. He begged some butterfly wings and a cup of spit from his neighbour Beauregard, and set about making his first hat. It was a remarkable creation, glued together with toadspit, and light as a feather. Jorge wore it to supper that night and drew many admiring looks, and some rude sniggers.

The way it is with creative people like Jorge, they are never satisfied, and he kept making more and more astonishing and outlandish hats, giving them away until every frog, toad, newt and lizard had a hat of his choice.

* *The Secret Loves of Madame Gigi*

He made a very special one for the Governor who wore it at Roll Call, and feeling ennobled by the distinguished hat was inspired to give a lecture entitled 'Developing your Potential'.

He meant well, of course, but some of the inmates had talents which were more in need of suppression than development; conmen and swindlers whose talents for deception needed re-directing into some influence for good.

Jorge and his hats proved to be a wonderful distraction from the monotony of prison life, and he drew many admirers clamouring for him to branch out into costume design, notably the Theatrical Society, which was planning a surprise production of 'The Great Escape' to celebrate the Governor's birthday. Jorge readily agreed to their request, on condition that he would be allowed to join the cast on the opening night. He set to work with a will. I was a bit suspicious of the intentions of the Theatrical Society, which was composed of all the worst thugs, muggers, rogues and bouncers in the prison, however, I gave them the benefit of the doubt and concentrated instead on preparations for the Governor's Birthday Party. Then a terrible thing happened.

My release date had arrived, and I hadn't noticed that my time was up. I had finished my sentence and was due to be returned to society immediately. It was a dreadful blow. What would happen to my kitchen, and to all my good work in the restaurant? The Governor and Chief Accountant shared my concern and were sorry to see me go. As a sincere reformer, the Governor could hardly say, "I hope to see you back here soon", although he wanted to.

I hope you will understand when you read this, that my subsequent actions were for the best reasons, and you will forgive me when I tell you that on my first day of freedom I assaulted a policeman, and was immediately arrested. They put me in a police cell while I awaited trial, with nothing but a daily newspaper to pass the time. I had to laugh when I read the headlines: **'Thespian thugs leg it'**. **'Red faces at prison'**. It seemed that the Theatrical Society had had a first night success with their 'Great Escape'.

The next morning I was in court facing my accuser, the unfortunate gendarme. The magistrate sentenced me to a further term in prison, claiming that I was a hardened criminal incapable of reform. This was music to my ears as it meant I could return to my beloved prison kitchen without the threat of early release hanging over me.

I was happy again. As the days passed, I noticed familiar faces returning as the Theatrical Society were recaptured one by one. But not Jorge. He got away.

Among the sorry group of recaptured Theatrical Society members was an unfamiliar face, a dark-skinned frog whose large, anxious eyes told me that this was his first time in prison. His name was

Ganesh Dedko, and he had been caught up in a police raid on the swamp where the escapees had been hiding.

Ganesh had a small business selling bee-stings to a foreign fast-foodery, and while delivering a batch of dried stingers to the muddy cavern where drainage workers, escaped convicts, and other shady characters gathered to exchange gossip and create rumours, the police swooped.

Ganesh's protestations of innocence fell on deaf ears. His lilting voice and foreign accent, combined with his dark looks were enough to condemn him. Guilty by Association was the police verdict, and the hapless Ganesh was thrown into jail with the others.

Having had some experience in the food trade, albeit slight, Ganesh applied to join me in the kitchens and, impressed by his polite manners and considerate nature, I took him on as a waiter. But not before finding out about his background. This is what he told me.

Ganesh Dedko

"I was born in a distant land, very different from this one, where the ground is hard, and baked red by a sun so hot that frogs have to bury themselves underground for months, to avoid being burned to death. Then the rains come, so violently that large boulders are washed away in the floods, and all the cracks and hollows in the ground fill up with cool water.

This is a good time for frogs, who emerge to a green world full of the most delicious flying insects and crawling bugs.

It is also a time when frog eggs turn into little tadpoles, who now enter a dangerous arena of swooping birds and hungry snakes.

I was one of those tadpoles, small, but full of wriggling energy and a will to survive. I was washed by the floods to a puddle near a ruined building by the village tank, where a poor beggar man huddled, sheltering from the rains.

With only the thought of evading death from the cruel beaks of crows in mind, I squirmed up the wall and hid in his turban where I remained, safe from all danger. I fed on the many flies and insects which seemed attracted to the turban, and before long, I grew big and strong.

My new companion found work in the forest, picking mangoes and packing them in boxes. Each mango was laid in a nest of pink tissue in the boxes, which were stacked on a cart awaiting transport to the town. Seeing my chance to travel, I hopped into one of the boxes, and fell asleep.

When I awoke I was in a foreign land, bumping along on the back of a truck. It was bewildering to watch the unfamiliar scenery go by. I saw great mountains, lakes, forests and finally, a swamp.

That's where I got off.

It was in this swamp that I began to make my own way in life. I struggled to learn the language of this country, but sadly missed the spicy insects of my native land. I was permanently hungry for the familiar stinging ants, wasps and small juicy bees, which I had so enjoyed at home. I started to collect crushed beetle wings, dried wasp stings, stickleback spines and the brittle bodies of certain rare

27

moths. Ground together, they made an aromatic and spicy powder, which I sold to adventurous cooks for their stews. It was while I was thus engaged that I was wrongfully arrested, and brought here."

Having listened to Ganesh's story, I was satisfied that he was an honest fellow, and together we went to the Governor to plead his case for release. The Governor was of the same opinion as me, but cautiously suggested giving him a trial period waiting at table, to see if he liked it sufficiently to remain in the prison.

A job is a job after all, he said.

Ganesh thought about this for a moment, and then agreed to the plan on condition he would be released periodically to collect ingredients for his spice powder. It was an excellent arrangement, and now Ganesh is a key member of my culinary team.

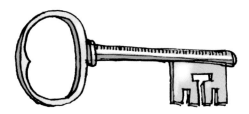

Toro the Trusty

After the fiasco of the Governor's birthday celebrations, there was an official crackdown on all activities organised by the inmates, which might lead to disturbances or breakouts. For this reason, official approval was only given to groups such as the Ikebana Club, The Hopscotch League, or the Staring Society. There was an absolute ban on all sports that could be performed above head height.

This was the Governor's strict rule, and any prisoner caught pole-vaulting, trampolining, or stilt walking would have to deal with Toro the Trusty, the only inmate trusted with the key to the prison, so that he could run errands for the Governor.

This individual was a large and intimidating bullfrog, with a gruff voice and an extensive vocabulary of swear words.

His function was to keep order among the contestants on Sports Day, to referee the games, urge on reluctant participants in physical contests, and bash those he didn't like. His guiding principle as a referee was 'If you can't be just, be arbitrary', and the result was that Toro's cronies always won.

By and large, the forgers, swindlers and con artists were not of the violent physical type favoured by Toro the Trusty, but they did have something he lacked - they were smart. And they hated him. They conspired to devise a plan to get rid of him for good, and soon they had the answer.

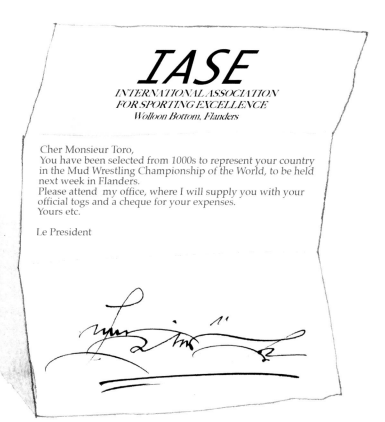

IASE

INTERNATIONAL ASSOCIATION
FOR SPORTING EXCELLENCE
Wolloon Bottom, Flanders

Cher Monsieur Toro,
You have been selected from 1000s to represent your country
in the Mud Wrestling Championship of the World, to be held
next week in Flanders.
Please attend my office, where I will supply you with your
official togs and a cheque for your expenses.
Yours etc.

Le President

A letter arrived one day, addressed to Toro, c/o The Prison. This was a rare occurrence, and it was by no means certain that Toro the Trusty could read. He showed the letter to me and asked my opinion on its content. The letter had an impressively official looking letterhead, and was printed in large legible type. It was from the President of the International Association for Sporting Excellence, and read as follows:

Cher Monsieur Toro,
You have been selected from 1000s to represent your country in the Mud Wrestling Championship of the World to be held next week in Flanders. Please attend my office, where I will supply you with your official togs, and a cheque for your expenses.
Yours, etc....

I advised Toro to keep the letter secret from the Governor, who might refuse him permission to attend this prestigious event, but to use his key to the prison door to slip out unnoticed and journey to Flanders. Toro could barely conceal his excitement at being selected to wrestle the top mud fighters of all nations, and one night, when the lizard guarding the gate was asleep on duty, he sneaked out, and we never saw him again.

We knew that Toro's privileged position as Trusty would be stripped from him if he ever returned, and he'd be given a severe punishment for abusing his trust. So we celebrated, and toasted the health of the forgers who had achieved such a satisfactory result.

Visiting Day

Visiting Day brought a collection of outsiders to the prison; relatives, friends, old partners in crime, and the Governor made them all welcome. The Chief Accountant arranged visiting hours to coincide with lunch and dinner times, so that the visitors were hungry on arrival, and were eager to dine in the smart Prison Restaurant, even though they were charged an admission fee, and the meal prices were high. Nobody complained, as the food was delicious, and very soon word spread that my restaurant was the best in the country.

The Governor and his Accountant got rich, and the restaurant became famous for attracting film and sports stars, opera singers, and all the rich celebrities in the land.

People could only get a booking for the restaurant if they could claim to be visiting a prisoner, and the inmates were deluged with letters from the rich and curious offering them bribes to let them use their names.

So everybody benefited.

Customers would arrive wide-eyed with excitement at the sight of so many criminals, and were thrilled to be served at table by a dangerous murderer or forger. I noticed with amusement a change in their attire; from the formal dinner dress worn on gala occasions, to a more casual look – tailored outfits featuring stripes and broad arrows. 'Prison chic' they called it, and the fashion magazines paid large sums of money to the Chief Accountant for permission to send their photographers and models to pose in our prison kitchen, with me and my helpers.

They even sent a journalist to interview my father, Gaston, who knew all about my life of crime, but nothing about my subsequent career in the prison kitchens. He was mortified to find that it was common knowledge his son was a jailbird, but also proud that I had done so well, and in the family tradition too. He wrote to me saying how pleased he and my mother, Gigi were at my redemption, and how they now forgave me for making their lives a misery when I was a child. To go from being a horrible little delinquent with no future other than a life of crime, to being a celebrated chef was, in their opinion, a miracle. He laid it on a bit thick, I thought, filling the letter with examples of my early misdemeanours, but in the end he grudgingly conceded that I was forgiven. Well thanks, Papa.

Estofado de Cucaracha

Another letter came, postmarked *Paraguas, Amazonia*. It was from Jorge, who had managed to return to his native jungle, and was currently under investigation for his part in the disappearance of the explorer, *Goulu Rana, last seen in the territory of the blue-skinned Amazonian poison arrow frogs. It was a cheerful letter, full of reminiscences about our times together in prison, and he had enclosed a small packet containing a spider web. This, he explained, was a rare and wonderful medicinal flavouring agent, which he had used to spice up Goulu's last meal. He suggested I use it in my celebrated *Estofado de Cucaracha*.

* *The Secret Loves of Madame Gigi*

35

I did as he said, and the effect was truly remarkable. After the first taste of my stew a strange thing happened to the diners.

They burst into laughter and clapped their hands as a firework display exploded upon them with scarlet snakes of fire, purple blossoms, rainstorms of silver sparks, whirlpools of molten gold spiralling down between glittering canyons of obsidian and melted emeralds. The tablecloths became undulating liquid ponds of quicksilver, and the cutlery took flight with wings of snakeskin and ice.

Some felt themselves streaking like kingfishers, encircling the world at unimaginable speeds, looking down on the ruins of ancient civilizations, oceans full of drowned cities, and endless plains of perfumed moss. Others became moles and tunnelled through diamond mines, caves spiny with iridescent stalactites, and deep bogs layered with helmeted conquistadors nattering in archaic Spanish.

After a while, the diners grew solemn, their eyes tight shut, and apart from the occasional contented burp, all was silence. They departed, shaken by the experience and vowing to return every year to partake of my magical *Estofado de Cucaracha*.

This was the high point of my culinary career, and the Governor recognised it. He summoned me to his office, and together with the Chief Accountant, made me a proposition.

"My dear friend, Gaspard," he said "the time has come which we all dreaded, and I'm sorry to tell you that tomorrow is your last day with us. Your sentence is finished, and we will soon be saying good-bye."

The pair of them sat in silence for a long minute, looking at my glum expression, and then burst into laughter. Seeing the consternation on my face, the Governor relented, and continued…

"However, the Chief Accountant and I would like to offer you the full-time post of Chef de Cuisine and Inspector of Prison Catering, with a handsome salary. What do you say to that?"

I felt dizzy, nearly fell on the floor, and finally stammered,

"I'll t-t-t-take it"

So there my story ends. And if you ever want to visit me at the prison, just look for the sign, it's bright green and can be seen for miles….

The end